Tales of Sweet Dreams

Playful Friend

Copyright Page

First Edition
Release Year 2024

INDEX

The Soft Cloud

Once upon a time, in the blue sky, there was a very soft and fluffy cloud. It was white like cotton and floated gently across the sky, as if it were dancing. This cloud was very special because it had an important job: to help babies sleep peacefully.

Every night, when the sun set and the sky darkened, the soft cloud began its walk. It floated slowly, very slowly, so as not to wake anyone. Gentle as a caress, it moved among the stars, who greeted it with a soft, bright light.

The soft cloud went from one side to the other, spreading its magic of sleep. Her sighs were like sweet songs that filled the air with calm and peace. As she passed near the houses, she sang in a soft voice: "Go to sleep, baby, go to sleep now, the night is beautiful, the night is peaceful."

Sometimes, she would approach the windows of the children's rooms. Very carefully, the soft cloud would extend a small piece of her cotton to give them a gentle hug. The babies would smile in their sleep and snuggle deeper into their beds, as the cloud continued on its journey.

Some nights, the moon would come out and accompany the cloud on his walk. The moon was also a great friend of babies and would whisper sweet words to them. "Good night, little ones," said the moon, shining with a very, very soft light. Together, the cloud and the moon made a perfect team to fill the night with calm and sweet dreams.

In the sky, there were also little stars that were twinkling, as if they wanted to help too. "Can I help you, cloud?" said the stars, shining with their light. The soft cloud smiled and said: "Of course, dear stars. Shine a little brighter so that all the babies have nice dreams."

And so the cloud continued on its journey, floating across the sky as if it were in a slow dance. Sometimes, the wind helped it, blowing slowly so that it could move effortlessly.

"Thank you, wind," said the soft cloud with a smile.

Little by little, the night became quieter, and the sky was filled with a silence as soft as a blanket. The cloud saw all the sleeping babies, with happy faces and relaxed bodies. Its work was done.

Then the cloud would take one last turn in the sky, feeling content and happy to have helped so many children to sleep. Then she would curl up in a corner of the sky, close her eyes and drift off to the gentle sleep of the night.

And so the soft cloud slept, waiting for another night to come, ready to begin its walk across the sky again, spreading peace and sweet dreams to all the babies.

The Sleeping Moon

Once upon a time, in the dark night sky, there was a very, very beautiful moon. It was round and big, with a soft, warm light. This moon loved to sleep, so much so that everyone in the sky called it the Sleepy Moon.

Every night, when the sun said goodbye, the moon appeared in the sky, ready for its night walk. But the moon had a secret: she loved to sleep! However, she knew that her job was important. She had to light up the sky so that all the babies could sleep peacefully and without fear.

The Sleepy Moon began her walk slowly, very slowly. She moved gently, almost as if she were floating in the air. Around her, many stars looked at her and said: "Good night, Sleepy Moon!" And the moon, with a smile, answered them: "Good night, little stars."

As the moon strolled across the sky, she greeted all the little animals who were also getting ready for sleep. She would dip down a little to greet the owl, who was always awake at night. "Hello, Mr. Owl," the moon would say. And the owl, with his big round eyes, would reply, "Good night, Sleepy Moon. Have a peaceful walk."

Then the moon saw the bunnies in the field, curled up in their beds of leaves. The bunnies would raise their ears when they saw the moonlight and say, "Thank you for shining on us, Sleepy Moon!" The moon smiled and continued on her way, slower than ever, because she was beginning to feel very, very sleepy.

As she moved forward, the moon looked into the windows of the houses, where the babies slept in their little beds. With great care, the moon peeked out and sent them a soft ray of light, like a luminous hug. The babies sighed in their dreams and smiled, feeling the quiet presence of the moon.

But suddenly the Sleepy Moon began to yawn. She was so tired! "Oh," whispered the moon, "I'm falling asleep... but I must keep shining." So she floated on, even though her eyes were slowly beginning to close. The moon daydreamed of fields of stars and pillows of clouds.

The stars, who were very good friends of the Sleeping Moon, noticed that she was very tired. "Dear Moon," said the stars, "let us help you. We too can shine a little brighter tonight, so that you can rest for a while."

The moon smiled and thanked her friends. "Thank you, little stars. I think I need a little rest." Then, she curled up in the sky and closed her little eyes, while the stars surrounded her and filled the sky with their light. With that starlight, the sky was more beautiful than ever, and all the babies were sleeping soundly.

So, the Sleepy Moon slept happily in the sky, knowing that her friends were taking care of everyone while she rested. Sometimes, she would wake up a little and look at the babies, who continued sleeping peacefully. Satisfied, she would close her eyes again, feeling the calm and peace of the night.

The Sleepy Moon dreamed of skies filled with soft light, of lullabies whispered by the wind, and of the love she felt for all the babies in the world. And when the sun began to rise, the moon gave one last yawn, bidding farewell to the sky until the next night.

And so, every night, the Sleepy Moon came out to walk and shine, with her sleepy eyes and soft light, watching over all those who slept and filling the world with sweet dreams.

The Whisper of the Wind

Once upon a time, there was a very soft and gentle wind that lived in the sky. This wind was not strong or loud, it did not blow the leaves or move the branches of the trees. On the contrary, this wind was a whisper, a sweet and quiet wind that only wanted to put everyone who heard it to sleep.

Every night, when the sun set and the stars began to shine, the wind would come out to wander through the world. Very carefully, it would begin to move slowly through the trees, singing a very soft and melodious song. The leaves of the trees, feeling the whisper of the wind, would sway silently, as if they were dancing a slow and calm dance.

The wind continued on its way, passing through the fields where the flowers were sleeping. As they felt the whisper of the wind, the petals of the flowers closed a little more, hugging each other to sleep. "Sweet dreams, little flowers," the wind whispered, and the flowers sighed softly, letting themselves be carried away by sleep.

Then the wind continued its journey to the rivers and streams, where the water sparkled in the moonlight. As the wind passed, it touched the water with its gentle fingers, creating little ripples that seemed like a song. “Rest, still water,” the wind said, and the river responded with a soft murmur, as if grateful for the wind’s company.

The wind, with its light movements, reached the high mountains, where owls and other nocturnal animals listened attentively. The owls found the whisper of the wind calming, and they closed their big eyes little by little, letting the wind lull them. “Good night, Mr. Owl,” said the wind, and the owl nodded, feeling sleep slowly enveloping him.

As the wind blew past, it also reached the windows of the houses, where children and babies slept in their beds. Carefully, the wind blew softly near the windows, singing its special tune. “Sleep, sleep, little baby, the wind will take care of you,” it whispered tenderly, and the babies sighed and snuggled into their little beds, lulled by the quiet sound of the wind.

Sometimes the wind would stop for a moment and look up at the sky, where the moon and stars were watching him lovingly. The moon, with its soft light, would smile at the wind and say, "Thank you, dear wind, for taking care of everyone while they sleep." The wind would smile back and reply to the moon, "It is a pleasure, dear moon. I want everyone to have peaceful and beautiful dreams."

Little by little, the wind continued its journey, spreading its soft whisper everywhere. It passed by the nests of the little birds, who slept embraced between its wings, and also by the fields where the small animals, such as rabbits and mice, rested curled up in their homes. Each of them, hearing the whisper of the wind, relaxed even more, letting sleep come in a peaceful and sweet way.

When the night was at its deepest and darkest, the wind gave a last whisper, soft as a caress. "Good night, everyone," it said, "rest well, and I will watch over your dreams." And so, all the little animals, the flowers, the trees and the babies slept soundly, feeling safe and happy thanks to the gentle wind.

At the end of the night, when the sun began to peek timidly over the horizon, the wind made one last turn around the world, making sure that everything was calm. Then, very slowly, it slipped away into the clouds, where it curled up to rest until the next night.

And so, the soft, calm wind slept too, with the satisfaction of having lulled everyone into a beautiful, peaceful sleep, waiting for the next nightfall to arrive so it could sing its sweet whisper again.

The Bright Star

Once upon a time, high up in the dark sky, there was a little star that shone brighter than all the others. This star was so special that everyone called it the Bright Star. It had a warm, soft light that lit up the sky, and it loved to watch the Earth from its place in space.

Every night, when the sun said goodbye and the moon rose in the sky, the Bright Star began its task. It was a very friendly and loving star, and its mission was to illuminate the dreams of all children and babies.

From its corner in the sky, the star watched over the houses, fields, forests and rivers, making sure that everything was quiet and peaceful.

Bright Star had many friends in the sky, like the other stars and the moon. They all said to her, "Thank you, Bright Star, for giving us your beautiful light." The star smiled and replied, "I like to light up the sky so that everyone can sleep peacefully."

One night, the Bright Star decided to do something special. He came a little closer to Earth, where he could see the babies and children sleeping in their little beds. He carefully sent a very soft beam of light through the windows and glided like a blanket of light around the little ones.

Feeling the star's ray, the babies sighed in their sleep and smiled. It was as if the soft light of the star gave them a warm hug and filled them with peace. The Bright Star felt happy to see the babies sleeping so peacefully, snuggled and safe in their beds.

As the night progressed, the star visited many places. It passed over the fields where the bunnies slept hidden among the flowers, and its soft light enveloped them like a caress. The bunnies huddled even closer, feeling safe under the star's light.

Then the Bright Star flew over the forest, where the birds slept in their nests and the little bears huddled in their caves. All the little animals felt the light of the star and slept soundly, as if a magical sleep had enveloped them. “Sweet dreams, my dear friends,” said the star in a voice as soft as a whisper.

As the star shone brightly, the moon came to her and said, “Dear Bright Star, your light is the most beautiful of all. Thank you for shining on everyone tonight.” Bright Star blushed a little, very happy that the moon appreciated her light, and replied, “It is my joy to see everyone resting under my light.”

Then, the Bright Star saw something special. From the sky, he saw a little boy looking up from his window. The boy looked very amazed, staring at the star with wide eyes. The Bright Star smiled down at him, and the boy waved to her with his little hand.

"Hello, little star," whispered the boy, "thank you for lighting up my night!" The star was so happy to hear this that it shone a little brighter, as if to say hello. The boy sighed happily and slowly closed his eyes, letting sleep envelop him. The Bright Star watched him until he was safely asleep, and then continued its walk across the sky.

The star knew that she had done something important: she had given peace and sweet dreams to all who slept under her light. With each ray, she made sure that the dreams were peaceful and beautiful, filled with peace and love. And so, the night continued, and the Bright Star continued on her mission, shining with love for all who slept.

Finally, when the night was almost over, the Bright Star took one last turn across the sky, making sure that everyone was fast asleep and happy. Then, she waved to her star friends and winked at the moon. "See you tomorrow, dear moon," said the star.

And when the sun began to peek over the horizon, the Bright Star slowly lowered its light, hiding in the sky until the next night. But it was always there, patiently waiting for the moment to light up the sky again and accompany everyone in their dreams.

So, every night, the Bright Star came out to shine, watching over everyone's dreams with its warm and loving light.

The Cotton Boat

Once upon a time, in a corner of the sky, there was a soft, fluffy cloud that looked very much like a little boat. This little cotton boat was so light that it floated effortlessly among the other clouds. Every night, when the moon appeared in the sky, the little cotton boat would prepare for a magical adventure, sailing among the stars.

This little boat had no oars or sails, but it had something even more special: the breeze of the night wind carried it gently wherever it wanted to go! When the sun said goodbye and the sky darkened, the wind whispered to the little cotton boat: "Are you ready to set sail?" And the little boat, excited, responded with a little rocking, as if to say "Yes!"

The little cotton boat's first stop was always the moon. The moon, big and bright, greeted him every night and said, "Welcome, little cotton boat. Where will you go tonight?" And the little boat smiled, happy to see the moon, and answered, "Tonight I want to travel far away, to bring sweet dreams to all the children of the world."

So the wind began to blow a little harder, and the little cotton boat began to move, gliding across the sky. It passed through a sea of stars, each one shining like a firefly in the night. The stars, seeing the little boat, greeted it and said, "Hello, little boat! Have a good voyage!" And the little cotton boat responded with a gentle rocking motion, grateful for their good wishes.

On its journey, the little boat would arrive at the houses where the children were sleeping peacefully in their beds. It would slowly approach the windows and, without making a sound, it would release a whisper of sweet dreams that would enter the rooms. "Dream of beautiful things, little one," the little boat seemed to say, while its soft cottony wake filled the air with peace and love.

Sometimes the little cotton boat would stop over a field full of sleeping flowers. As it passed over them, it would drop a little of its softness, as if giving them a fluffy blanket to protect them from the cold of the night. The flowers would curl up even closer, happy to feel the warmth of the little boat, and their petals would shine a little under the moonlight.

The little boat also visited the rivers, which shone in the darkness like silver ribbons. It floated on the water, where the fish slept peacefully. As it passed over the river, the little cotton boat released sparkles, which made the water shine as if it were full of little stars. The fish, feeling the soft glow, sighed in their dreams, thanking the little boat for its visit.

The wind, guiding the little boat, said softly: "Are you having fun, little boat?" And the little cotton boat, happy and full of happiness, rocked as a sign that yes, it was enjoying every moment of its night journey. There was nothing it liked more than to spread peaceful and soft dreams.

After visiting many places and leaving his magic touch, the little cotton boat felt very happy. He knew that his mission was special, that every child, every flower and every little fish in the river slept better thanks to his visit. The little boat, although small, had a huge heart and was full of love.

Finally, as the night began to end and the sun began to rise, the little cotton boat headed back toward the moon to say goodbye. The moon, which had been watching him since his first step, said to him in a kind voice: “Good job, little cotton boat. Thank you for bringing peace and sweet dreams."

The little boat rocked once more, happy to have fulfilled its mission. It knew that it would soon dissolve with the morning sun, but it did not matter, because it would return each night to bring its softness to all corners of the sky and the earth.

Thus the little cotton boat gently disappeared with the first ray of sunshine, leaving the sky clear and bright for a new day. But, in the hearts of all those he had visited that night, a small trace of his sweet and fluffy dreams remained, waiting for him to return with the arrival of the next night.

And so, every night, the little cotton boat would set sail again, delivering peaceful, loving dreams to all who slept beneath the sky.

The Dreaming Bunny

Once upon a time, there was a little bunny named Tino, who lived in a green field full of flowers, trees, and soft grass. Tino was a very special bunny, because he had a habit of dreaming about wonderful things every night. Everyone in the field called him “the Dreamy Bunny" because his dreams were so beautiful that they seemed magical.

Every night, when the sun went down and the sky was filled with stars, Tino would curl up in his nest made of leaves and grass. He would curl up so tightly that he looked like a soft, white ball. He would close his eyes, sigh deeply, and slowly begin to dream.

In his dreams, Tino traveled to incredible places. One night he dreamed that he could fly like a bird, spreading his little legs like wings. He felt the fresh wind on his face and saw how the field and the flowers became smaller and smaller. It was so exciting! Tino glided between the clouds, waving at the stars that looked at him curiously from high up in the sky.

One night, Tino dreamed that he was in a forest of giant carrots. The carrots were so tall that they looked like trees, and their green leaves formed a large shadow where Tino could rest. The dreaming bunny approached a carrot, hopped around, and took a bite. It was delicious! It was the perfect place for a bunny like him. Tino hopped from one carrot to another, laughing with joy, with his belly full and happy.

But there was one night in particular that Tino remembered fondly. It was the night he dreamed that he could jump to the moon. In his dream, the moon shone like a giant ball of cheese in the sky. Tino looked at the moon and thought, "It's so beautiful! I want to jump up there!" So in his dream, Tino took a giant leap, higher than ever before. He jumped and jumped until he reached the moon.

When Tino reached the moon, he found it to be a soft, shiny place, full of little stones that seemed to shine like diamonds. There, on the moon, Tino found other bunnies who were also dreaming and jumping around. They all welcomed him, and together they played and ran around, leaving little footprints in the shiny moon dust.

Sometimes Tino dreamed that he could talk to the stars. In one of those dreams, a very small, bright star came to him and said, “Hello, Tino, would you like to know the secrets of the sky?" Tino nodded, and the star led him along a path of light to a place full of constellations. There, the star showed him figures made of other stars that looked like animals and magical shapes.

The star told him: “Every night, we shine light on you from above so that you have sweet and wonderful dreams, little bunny.” Tino felt very grateful and happy knowing that the stars were watching over him and giving him that special light in his dreams.

One night, Tino dreamed that he was swimming in a river of milk. It was a soft, white river, and he let himself be carried along by its waters, floating like a little boat. From time to time, he would jump out of the water, feeling the freshness and laughing with bubbles that came out around him. It was such a sweet dream that, when he woke up, Tino licked his whiskers, remembering the sweetness of that river of milk.

Every night, Tino had a different dream. But all of those dreams had one thing in common: they were dreams filled with peace, joy, and magical adventures. When he woke up in the morning, Tino felt happy and rested. He looked up at the blue sky, remembering his dreams, and felt that the world was a place full of wonders to discover.

His friends from the countryside, like Paco the mouse and Lili the squirrel, always asked him: "What did you dream about last night, Tino?" And Tino, with a big smile, told them about all his adventures. His friends listened in wonder, imagining everything Tino told them.

As evening fell, Tino returned to his nest, snuggled up warm and prepared for another night of dreams. He closed his eyes, sighed deeply, and let his dreams take him to those magical places where only he could go.

And so, night after night, Dreamy Bunny continued to travel in his dreams, jumping among the stars, swimming in rivers of milk, and exploring forests of giant carrots.

The River Nanny

Once upon a time, in a quiet corner of the forest, there was a clear and serene river that flowed gently between the trees and flowers. This river was very special, because every night, when the sky darkened and the moon began to shine, the river began to sing a soft and sweet lullaby that filled the air with peace.

The sound of its slowly flowing water made everyone in the forest feel calm and ready for sleep. Small animals, such as bunnies, squirrels and birds, would come to the riverbank to listen to its soft song. It was a melody that drifted like water, slow and whispering, like a gentle wind hugging it.

Every night, just as the first star appeared in the sky, the river would begin to sing. His song spoke of beautiful dreams, of soft clouds, and of stars that watched over the sky. He said secret words that only the little animals in the forest understood, words that told them that everything was okay and that they could rest without worry.

The bunnies huddled among the tree roots, listening to the river's song as they closed their eyes. Their ears moved gently to the rhythm of the melody, and little by little, they fell into a deep, peaceful sleep. Each note of the river's song seemed to caress their fur and say, "Sleep, little bunny, and I will take care of you."

By the riverside, there were also many flowers that leaned forward as if they were listening to the lullaby. The daisies, violets, and sunflowers closed their petals slowly, as if they were huddling, listening to every word that the river whispered to them. The lullaby was so sweet that it seemed as if even the leaves of the trees were singing it softly when the wind passed through them.

A family of ducklings living in the water also gathered together every night to listen to the lullaby of the river. The mother duck would arrange her ducklings next to each other, and they, with their bright and curious eyes, would snuggle up to her side. Little by little, the ducklings would also close their eyes, lulled by the song of the river, which seemed like a blanket of soft water that enveloped and cared for them.

Deep in the forest, the owls listened attentively from the high branches of the trees. Although they were nocturnal and did not sleep like the other little animals, they also liked the river's song very much. The owls moved their heads, accompanying the music with their big eyes, and every now and then, they joined in the song with their soft "uh-uh", as if they wanted to thank the river for its beautiful melody.

When the moon was full, the river seemed to sing even louder, as if it wanted everyone in the forest to hear its lullaby and have sweet dreams. Fireflies would start to shine around the river, lighting up the water like little stars. They too would move to the rhythm of the music, dancing gently in the air as they illuminated the lullaby's path.

There was a little green frog who always jumped to the edge of the river to listen to the song. The frog, very excited, closed his eyes and breathed deeply, feeling how each note filled him with tranquility. Sometimes, the frog even daydreamed, imagining that the music took him to distant worlds where only peace existed.

And so, every night, the river continued to sing its lullaby, while all the little animals in the forest fell into a deep sleep. The little birds huddled in their nests, the little squirrels curled up in their little houses in the trees, and even the insects rested under the leaves. The river's lullaby was like a promise, a love song that watched over everyone and gave them sweet, peaceful dreams.

As dawn came and the sun began to rise, the river's song grew softer, like a whisper, until it finally stopped. All the animals in the forest woke up happy and full of energy, knowing that the river had given them a night full of peace and sweet dreams.

And so the river continued to sing night after night, watching over all of his friends in the forest, and reminding them that they would always be safe under the starry sky and the moon.

The Sun That Sets

Once upon a time, in a huge, bright sky, there was a round, warm sun called Solín. Solín was very special, because every day he illuminated the whole world with his golden rays. With them, he made the trees, flowers and animals wake up happy. The sky was clear and beautiful when Solín was up, and the whole forest seemed to dance under his light.

Solín began his day very early, rising from the horizon and stretching out his rays. “Good morning, world,” said Solín with a warm smile. His rays gently touched the leaves of the trees, and they moved to the rhythm of his light. The little birds, feeling Solín's warmth, came out of their nests and began to sing, filling the air with joy.

The little rabbit, Hop, came out of his burrow, hopped around, and said to Solín: "Good morning, Solín! Thank you for your beautiful light!" Solín was happy to see everyone enjoying his glow, and he made sure that every corner of the forest had a little bit of his golden light.

Throughout the day, Solín continued to shine and move slowly in the sky. He went from one side to the other, as if he were on a long walk, watching everything that was happening on earth. He saw squirrels jumping from one tree to another, bees buzzing around the flowers, and ducklings splashing in the lake. Everything under his light was colorful and cheerful.

But after a long and beautiful day, Solín was starting to feel a little tired.

He had been shining for hours and hours, and now he felt it was time to rest. So he began to move slowly towards the other side of the sky, the side where night fell. The animals looked at Solín and knew that he was about to "go to bed," because the day was coming to an end.

As Solín descended, the sky began to change color. First, the sky turned orange, like a big soft blanket. Then, the orange mixed with a pink color, and the entire forest seemed to be wrapped in a warm, pink embrace.

Finally, the sky turned a deep purple, and Solín smiled happily, knowing that he had done a great job brightening the day.

The little fox Mico looked at Solín from the edge of the forest and said: "Thank you for such a beautiful day, Solín! Rest well!" Solín, now low in the sky, responded with his soft light: "Good night, little friends. Tomorrow I will return to fill you with light again."

When Solín was almost on the horizon, his last rays touched the lake, and the water sparkled as if it had little stars on its surface. The ducklings on the lake saw how the sky darkened and the water changed color. They knew it was time to rest, and they huddled close to their mother duck, happy and safe under the last glow of Solín.

Finally, Solín disappeared behind the mountains, and the sky became dark and calm. But before leaving completely, Solín left a last whisper: "Good night, everyone. Tomorrow I will return, and my light will shine again." The animals of the forest smiled, and closed their eyes with a happy heart, knowing that Solín always returned to brighten their days.

So, as the moon rose in the sky and the stars began to shine, all the animals fell into a deep, peaceful sleep. They knew that at dawn, Solín would return with his warm, golden light to give them another day full of adventure and joy.

And so, night after night, Solín rested to wake up with energy, ready to light up the world once again.

The Stars That Tell Stories

Once upon a time, in the deep, dark night sky, there lived a very special group of stars. These stars not only shined and adorned the sky; they also had a magical secret: they knew how to tell stories! Every night, when the sun went to sleep and the sky became dark, the stars began to shine brighter and prepared to tell their stories to the whole world.

There were big stars and small ones, some with golden lights and others with silver lights. They all made patterns in the sky, and these patterns were called constellations. One night, when the forest was quiet and all the little animals were ready to sleep, the stars decided to tell a special story.

The first star to speak was Goldenstar, the brightest of them all. Goldenstar looked down and saw a group of bunnies huddled in their nests. Their golden light softly illuminated the forest, like a lantern in the night.

“Once upon a time,” Goldstar began, “there was a little rabbit who wanted to jump to the moon.” The bunnies listened intently, imagining the rabbit jumping so high, almost touching the sky! Goldstar told how the brave little rabbit had jumped over rivers and mountains, always with the moon as his guide.

Then the next star, named Silverstar, spoke up. Silverstar was very wise and always had stories full of magic. In her soft, sweet voice, she said, “My story is about a little girl who followed the fireflies to find a treasure hidden in the forest."

The squirrels and the little birds listened from their nests, imagining the forest filled with dancing lights. Silverstar told how the little girl had followed the glow of the fireflies to a secret clearing, where she found a shiny stone that could make her dreams come true. The squirrels looked at each other with dreamy eyes, wondering if they would ever see such a magic stone.

Then another little playful star, called Leaping Star, began her story. Leaping Star always told funny stories. “Once upon a time, there was a very curious fish who wanted to learn how to fly,” she began. The little animals in the river listened from the water, very interested in the story.

Leaping Star told how the little fish jumped higher and higher, wanting to see the sky from above. In the end, the little fish did not learn to fly, but he did learn to jump so high that he could see the clouds from the water.

The little fish in the river laughed and clapped their hands imagining the little fish's big jumps.

Then the oldest star of all, called Grandma Star, began her story. Her voice was calm and wise, and every time she spoke, everyone listened in silence. "This is a story about a tree that grew and grew until it touched the clouds," said Grandma Star.

The trees in the forest listened intently, very excited by the story. Grandma Star told how this special tree wanted to be so tall that it could see the whole world from the sky. Every night, the tree stretched its branches a little higher, getting closer and closer to the stars.

Grandma Estrella finished her story by saying that although the tree never touched the clouds, it was always happy, growing a little taller each day. The trees in the forest were inspired by her story and dreamed of growing as tall as that brave tree.

When each star finished its story, the sky was full of bright lights. The stars shone brighter than ever, as if each story had made them shine even brighter. The little animals in the forest, one by one, closed their eyes, feeling happy and safe under the sky full of stories.

Every night, the stars told new stories, and the little animals waited anxiously for nightfall to hear the stories of their friends in the sky. Thus, under the starry blanket, everyone in the forest learned and dreamed, thanks to the stars that told their magical stories every night.

The Rustling of the Leaves

Once upon a time, there was a very, very big forest, full of tall, leafy trees. In that forest, the leaves of the trees always had something special to say. Each leaf, no matter its size or color, had a hidden secret. When the wind blew gently, the leaves began to move and make a special sound, a soft rustling that filled the forest with magic.

Little bunny Cloud loved to listen to the rustling of the leaves. Every night, when the sun went down and the wind began to blow, Cloud would go to his favourite tree, an old and wise oak tree that had been in the forest for many years. He would curl up on the ground, close his eyes and listen to the rustling that travelled through the branches.

That night, the wind was gentle and the leaves began to move slowly, as if they were dancing in the air. Cloud listened attentively, and then, the leaves began to tell a story!

"Once upon a time," the leaves whispered, "there was a little mouse called Tico, who dreamed of seeing the world from the top of a tree." Cloud snuggled closer and listened excitedly. Tico was a very curious little mouse, but he had never climbed a tree before because he was a little afraid.

The leaves continued to tell: "One day, Tico looked up and saw the branches of the tree moving in the wind. The leaves were shining in the sun, and Tico thought they looked like little green stars. So, he decided it was time to give it a try."

Nube imagined the little mouse Tico, small and brave, slowly climbing up the tree trunk. The leaves, with their soft whispers, told how Tico climbed carefully, feeling the bark of the tree under his little paws. He climbed and climbed, looking around, and every time he felt afraid, he heard the whispers of the leaves, which told him: "Don't worry, Tico, keep going."

Little by little, Tico reached the first branch of the tree. He felt very proud of himself, and from there he looked down and saw the whole forest spread out around him. The colors were beautiful, and Tico felt as if he was flying in a magical place.

But Tico had not yet reached the top, and the little mouse wanted to reach the top. Carefully, he climbed onto the next branch, and then another, and another. The leaves accompanied him at every step, whispering words of encouragement and telling him that he was very close to his dream.

"When Tico finally reached the last branch, the wind blew hard and all the leaves on the tree made a great rustling sound, celebrating his bravery," the leaves told Nube. "From up there, Tico saw the sky, the sun and the clouds floating in the air. He felt very happy and grateful to the leaves, who had encouraged him to fulfill his dream."

Nube listened to the end of the story with a smile, feeling very happy for the little mouse Tico. He knew that the leaves were story whisperers and that, every night, they had different stories to tell.

The wind continued to blow softly, and the leaves continued to move on the branches, filling the air with magical whispers. That night, Nube closed his eyes under his favorite tree, imagining that he too was ascending to heaven like the little mouse Tico, surrounded by leaves and whispers.

And so, while the forest slept under the starry sky, the leaves continued to whisper their tales, filling every corner with stories that only the animals of the forest could hear.

The Sweet Wave

Once upon a time, on a quiet and beautiful beach, there was a very special wave that everyone called the Sweet Wave. The Sweet Wave was different from all the other waves in the sea. Instead of breaking hard on the shore, it came soft and delicate, as if it wanted to caress the sand with a very, very tender hug.

Every morning, as the sun rose and the sky filled with golden light, Sweet Wave would wake up. He would stretch, make a soft “shhh, shhh” noise, and get ready for his day.

Sweet Wave loved to watch the children playing on the beach, the seagulls flying in the sky, and the little fish swimming near the shore.

One day, while Sweet Wave was resting on the shore, he heard a little crab named Pico sighing very sadly. Pico was on the sand, looking out to sea with a worried face. Sweet Wave, curious, decided to approach him and ask him what was wrong.

—Why are you sad, little crab? —whispered Sweet Wave in her soft, sweet voice.

Pico looked at the wave and said:

— I want to learn to swim in the deep sea, but I'm a little scared. The waves are very big and fast.

Sweet Wave smiled tenderly and said to Pico:

— Don't worry, my little friend. I'm a very gentle wave. If you want, I can help you swim a little and show you the sea from up close.

Pico was relieved to hear that and decided to give it a try. With his little paws, he climbed onto the crest of Sweet Wave, and it began to move slowly, taking him for a ride on the water. Pico felt the sea under his little paws and the cool wind caressing his shell. It was a wonderful feeling!

The Sweet Wave carried him slowly, teaching him how to move through the water without being afraid. As they moved forward, they passed some bright little fish swimming in circles. The little fish greeted Pico and invited him to play. He was happy, and for the first time he felt safe and brave.

As Pico and Sweet Wave continued their walk, they found a starfish named Lia, who was resting on a rock. Lia looked at Pico and said:

— How brave you are, Pico! I have never dared to go so far from the shore.

Pico smiled and told her that Sweet Wave was helping him to get to know the sea. Lia was encouraged and asked Sweet Wave to take her on a ride too. Sweet Wave, happy to help, invited Lia to get on. Now Pico and Lia were riding together on the gentle wave, looking at the sea from above and laughing happily.

After a while, Sweet Wave showed them a part of the sea where the water was so clear that they could see everything at the bottom:

colorful stones, small snails, and even a puffer fish that swelled up like a round balloon. Pico and Lía looked at everything with amazed eyes, discovering things they had never seen from the shore.

Finally, the Sweet Wave brought them back to shore. Pico and Lia climbed down carefully and thanked the Sweet Wave for the special ride. They felt happy and brave, knowing that even though the sea could be big and mysterious, they could always count on the gentle Sweet Wave to guide them.

Every day after that adventure, Pico and Lia would return to the beach and look for Sweet Wave. Sometimes they would climb up to its crest and just drift along, and other times they would stay on the shore, listening to the soft "shhh, shhh" it made when it reached the sand.

Sweet Wave became the best friend of all the little inhabitants of the beach. She was always there, gentle and patient, ready to help any little friend who wanted to get to know the sea. And so, every night, when the sun was setting, Sweet Wave would say to everyone: "See you tomorrow," promising them a new day of adventures and sweet whispers in the sea.

And while the moon lit up the sky, the Sweet Wave continued its quiet dance, waiting for its little friends for the next adventure.

The Night Butterfly

In the silent forest full of soft shadows, there lived a little butterfly that only appeared when the sun set and the moon rose in the sky. This butterfly, which everyone called the Night Butterfly, was very special. Unlike the butterflies that flew during the day, she had dark wings with small bright dots, as if she carried the starry sky on her back.

Every night, when the moon lit up the forest, the Night Moth would wake up. First, it would gently stretch its antennae and wings, as if it were greeting the stars. Then, it would delicately take flight, making no noise, gliding between the sleeping trees and flowers.

The Night Moth loved to explore the forest in silence, for at night everything was quiet and calm. One night, as she was flying near a moonlit clearing, she heard a soft rustling. She looked around and, on a small leaf, she saw a small, sad-looking firefly.

—Why are you here all alone and so quiet? —the Night Moth asked her in a sweet voice.

The firefly sighed and explained:

—Today is the brightest night of all, and all my friends are playing in the sky, but I can't fly as high as them. I always stay down here, and I feel a little lonely.

The Night Butterfly smiled softly, and in a soft voice said to him:

— Don't be sad, my little friend. I fly low too, and if you want, we can explore the forest together. There are many beautiful things to see at night, and the moon is always with us.

The firefly, whose name was Lila, was encouraged by the idea and climbed onto the leaf. From there, the Night Moth invited her to come with her. Lila turned on her little light, and together they began to explore the forest, softly lighting the way.

As they flew, they found a spider web that was shining with dewdrops, like a pearl necklace. Lilac and the Moth came to look at it, admiring how the drops sparkled in the moonlight. Then they heard the rustling of leaves and saw a little mouse coming out of its house under a tree.

—Hello! —said the little mouse with a smile—. I have never seen such a beautiful butterfly at night. And you, little firefly, shine like a star.

Lila and the Night Moth were flattered and continued their flight, enjoying the silence and peace of the forest. As they went along, the Night Moth showed them some of her secret places: a flower that only opened in the dark and a calm lake where the stars were reflected in the water, creating a double sky.

The Lilac Firefly was so happy that she began to shine even brighter, and so, together with the Night Butterfly, they formed a small path of light that guided all the nocturnal animals.

The owl, who was watching from a tree branch, said to them:

— Thank you for bringing so much beauty to the night. I always look out at the forest, but tonight it looks especially beautiful thanks to you two.

Night Butterfly and Lilac smiled at each other, knowing that they were sharing the magic of the night with all of their friends.

Finally, as the stars began to fade and the sky announced the arrival of the sun, the Night Moth took Lilac back to her leaf, where she would rest until the next night.

— Thank you for this wonderful adventure —said Lila, yawning—. I saw things tonight that I will never forget.

The Night Moth gently caressed her with her wings and whispered:

— There is always magic in the night, my dear friend. You just have to know how to look.

And so, as the first ray of sunlight appeared on the horizon, the Night Moth said goodbye to Lila and flew to her secret corner in the forest to rest.

And from that day on, every time the sun set and the moon lit up the sky,

Lila knew that her friend the Night Butterfly would be there, ready to take her to explore the magical world of the night.

The Star Bear

Once upon a time, high up on a quiet mountain, there lived a little bear named Starlet. This bear was special because every night he would climb up to the top of the mountain to look at the stars. Starlet loved to see the dark sky filled with bright little dots.

From a very young age, Estrellito was fascinated by the stars. Every night, when the sun set and the moon began to light up the forest, he would leave his cave and walk to the top of the mountain to look at the sky. Sitting on a rock, Estrellito would look at the stars with wide eyes full of wonder.

One night, as Little Star was looking up at the sky, he noticed that one star seemed to be twinkling brighter than the others. The star was big and bright, and its light seemed to move, as if it were calling to him. Little Star stood up from his rock and, with a big smile, waved at the star.

—Hello, bright star! —said Starlet happily. —Why do you look so pretty tonight?

The star shone even brighter and, to Estrellito's surprise, answered him in a soft and friendly voice:

— Hello, little bear. My name is Lucia, and I am a star that watches over the dreams of all the little bears. Every night, I shine so that little bears like you can dream of beautiful things.

Little Star was excited. He had never talked to a star before, let alone one that looked after dreams. He felt very special to think that this star was there, shining just for him and the other bears.

— That's wonderful, Lucia! —said Estrellito, moving his little paws excitedly—. I'd love for you to tell me more about stars and dreams.

Lucia, the star, began to tell him stories about the sky. She told him about the constellations, those groups of stars that form shapes. She told him about a big bear in the sky, called the Big Dipper, who is always there to guide little bears like him. Little Star looked where Lucia was pointing and saw how the stars formed a kind of big bear.

Little Star was amazed. He had never realized that the sky was full of figures and secrets. As he listened to Lucia, his heart filled with joy and peace.

Then, Lucia said to him:

— You know, Starlet? When a little bear like you wants something really badly, he can make a wish upon the stars, and if he wishes for it with all his heart, the stars listen and can make that wish come true.

Little Star closed his eyes and thought of a wish. He dreamed of meeting other bears and sharing adventures with them. Although he loved the nights in the mountains, sometimes he felt a little lonely.

Very carefully, Star whispered her wish:

— Dear stars, I wish I had friends to share my nights in the mountains and watch the sky together.

Lucia listened to Estrellito's wish and, with a special glow, said to him:

— Don't worry, little one. The stars listen to all sincere wishes. You just have to wait patiently and, one day, you will have the friends you want.

Little Star smiled and looked at the sky once more before returning to his cave. That night, he slept soundly, and in his dreams, he saw a forest full of little bears like him, all looking at the sky together.

The next day, when the sun was already high and Little Star was picking berries in the forest, he heard a sound in the bushes. He stopped and looked curiously, and to his surprise, he saw two little bears, as small and curious as he was.

—Hello! —the bears said, smiling—. Our names are Luna and Sol. We like to explore the forest. Would you like to play with us?

Little Star couldn't believe it. Her wish had come true! She jumped for joy and answered them:

— Yes, of course! I would love to play and show you the place where I see the stars every night.

That night, Starlet took his new friends, Moon and Sun, to the top of the mountain. The three little bears sat together on the rock, looking up at the star-filled sky. Starlet told them about Lucy and the Big Dipper, and the three little bears imagined that they could see animal shapes and figures in the sky.

From then on, every night, Estrellito, Luna and Sol climbed the mountain together. Lucia and the other stars shone for them, creating a sky full of stories and dreams. The three friends hugged each other under the starry sky, feeling that the forest, the mountain and the stars were their home.

And so, the Night Butterfly joined them in their dreams, guarding their wishes and their friendship, while they slept under the blanket of an eternal sky.

Milton Keynes UK
Ingram Content Group UK Ltd.
UKHW030859151124
451262UK00001B/36

9 798227 089649